Written by Peter Bently
Illustrated by Simon Mendez

First published by Parragon in 2011

Parragon
Queen Street House
4 Queen Street
Bath BA1 1HE, UK

ISBN 978-1-4454-3019-5

Printed in China

Muddypaws

Goes to School

PaRragon

Bath • New York • Singapore • Hong Kong • Cologne • Delhi
Melbourne • Amsterdam • Johannesburg • Auckland • Shenzhen

Ben and his puppy, Muddypaws, did everything together.
They played inside...

they explored outside...

and at the end of the day they cuddled up together.

Wherever Ben went, Muddypaws went too.

"Except for school," smiled Ben, as Muddypaws **burst** a bubble.

"And my bath!"

The next day, Ben was late for school.
"See you later, Muddypaws!" he cried.
Uh-oh! Ben forgot to shut the gate!

Wherever Ben goes, I go, too!

When Muddypaws padded into school, he couldn't see
Ben anywhere.

He frolicked merrily in the nature corner...

and then **lolloped** off to the painting corner.

SQUISH! went the red.

SQUIRT! went the yellow and green.

SQUIRT! went the blue.

What fun! thought Muddypaws.

"What a mess!" gasped the teacher.
But where was Muddypaws?

Muddypaws was looking for Ben in the schoolyard.
He didn't find Ben, but he did find a shovel.
But I can dig with my paws! he thought.

SCRITCH–SCRATCH!

SCRITCH–SCRATCH!

SCRITCH–SCRATCH!

Muddypaws dug and dug and dug.

Digging is hard work! yawned Muddypaws. Here's a nice, cozy place for a nap.

"Oh no!" gasped the teacher at recess. "Who has made all this mess? They've buried all the flowers in the sand!"

Muddypaws woke up with a bump.

wheeeeeee!! he thought.

I'm going for a ride! Maybe I'll find Ben on the way.

Ben was upside down on the jungle gym.
"Hey!" he said. "That wagon has a tail!"

But when he looked again the wagon was empty.

Muddypaws had sniffed something tasty.

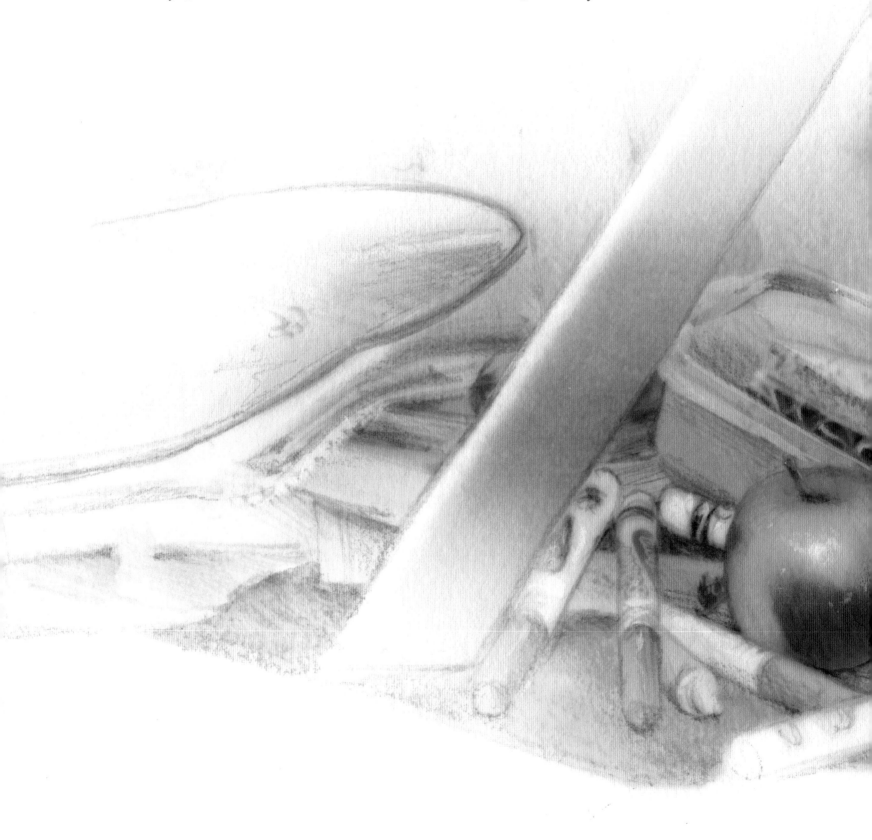

"Yummy! A snack!"

Back in class, Amy started to sob.
"She's lost her toy puppy!" said Ben.
"Don't worry, Amy," said the teacher. "We'll all help you find it."

The children hunted inside...

…and outside.

"Here it is, Amy!" cried Ben. But what was Amy giggling at?

"You found my puppy!" smiled Amy.

"And you found mine!" laughed Ben. "Hello Muddypaws! What are you doing at school?"

Muddypaws trotted home with Ben, proudly
wearing the star that the teacher had made him.

"My teacher says your name should be Mischief, not Muddypaws!" said Ben.

"But I love you just the same!"